This very lovely book belongs
to me and my name is:

Ellie Mae — ALWAYS try your best AT

EVERYTHING YOU DO... AND REMEMBER THAT
GOD HAS MADE YOU WITH A VERY SPECIAL PURPOSE
JUST THE WAY HE WANTS
YOU TO BE... YOU ARE
PERFECT IN HIS EYES AND
IN OURS! I LOVE
MOMMY &
DADDY

HAPPY EASTER!

Illustrated by Shelagh McNicholas
Written by Gaby Goldsack

First published by Parragon in 2009

Parragon
Queen Street House
4 Queen Street
Bath BA1 1HE, UK

ISBN 978-1-4075-4467-0

Manufactured in China

Please retain this information for future reference.

Angel

Lily and the Special Gift

Bath New York Singapore Hong Kong Cologne Delhi Melbourne

One day, Sophia went to play in the park behind her house. Her friends, Abby and Katie, were doing cartwheels on the grass. It didn't look hard, so Sophia decided to try one herself.

She held her arm above her head and pointed her left toe in front of her. "This is going to be perfect," she thought as she threw herself onto her hands and…

…crumpled into an untidy pile.

"Have another try," said Abby kindly.
"It takes a little practice to get it right."
So Sophia tried again...

And again...

...And again.

But Sophia just couldn't get it right.
She wasn't any good at cartwheels.
After a while, Sophia gave up trying,
so Abby and Katie played on their own.

Sophia felt very sad.
She did what she always did
when she felt sad. She went
to sit in her secret place
beneath the willow tree in
the corner of her yard.

Sophia rested her
chin on her hands
and looked down
at the ground.

"It's just not fair," she said out loud. "Abby and Katie are always so good at everything. I'm not good at anything. I wish I could be more like them."

As she spoke, there was a flash of light and a beautiful lady appeared. Sophia was so surprised that she tumbled backward.

"Here, let me help you," said the lady, in the sweetest voice Sophia had ever heard. She gently helped Sophia to her feet. Sophia noticed that the lady had soft, downy wings. A ring of light shimmered above her head, but Sophia didn't feel afraid at all.

"Who are you?" asked Sophia shyly.

"My name's Lily," replied the lady. "I'm your guardian angel."

"I didn't know I had a guardian angel!" gasped Sophia.

"Of course you do," smiled the angel. "Everyone has a guardian angel."

"Come with me," said Angel Lily.
"I want to show you some things."

Angel Lily took Sophia by the hand and led her back to the park. Abby and Katie had finished doing cartwheels.

Abby was playing with her jumping rope, and Katie was
bouncing a basketball.

"Hello," said Sophia. "Look, I've got a guardian angel!"

Abby and Katie didn't reply, or even look at Sophia.
They just carried on talking to each other.

"That's strange," said Sophia.
"Why are my friends ignoring me?"

"They aren't ignoring you. They can't see or hear us,"
Angel Lily explained kindly. "I'm your personal guardian angel,
so you are the only one who can see me. And when you're
with me, no one can see or hear you either—you're invisible."

Sophia was busy thinking about how strange it was to be invisible, when she heard a yelp.

She span around and saw Abby sitting on the grass, with her jumping rope tangled around her ankles.

Abby untangled herself and got up. She started jumping again, but a few seconds later she tripped over the jumping rope and giggled.

"Abby tries her best but she's not great at jumping," said Angel Lily.

As Abby jumped clumsily away, Angel Lily turned Sophia around. Katie was trying to throw her ball through a basketball hoop, but she wasn't having much luck.

Sometimes it went to the left.

Sometimes it went to the right.

Sometimes it missed the net entirely.

"Katie is wonderful at cartwheels, but she isn't very good at basketball," said Angel Lily. And just at that moment, Katie's ball bounced off the net toward Sophia. She ducked out of the way just in time.

Angel Lily led Sophia back to her yard. Sophia's dad was standing beside the vegetable plot, scratching his head.

He was staring at some shriveled plants. He couldn't understand what had happened.

Sophia tugged at the angel's hand. "Dad's a great gardener," she whispered. "But sometimes things just go wrong."

"Exactly," smiled the angel. "You see, no one is perfect. All anyone can do is try their best."

Sophia wandered back to the willow tree, daydreaming about trying her best. She was so busy thinking that it took her a while to realize that she was alone. Sophia looked around, but Angel Lily had completely vanished.

"Maybe she was never here, at all," thought Sophia. "Maybe I just imagined her." Then she noticed something lying on the ground. It was a necklace with a shining star-shaped pendant.

Sophia smiled and fastened the necklace around her neck. Perhaps she hadn't imagined her guardian angel after all.

Sophia felt so happy that she ran out to the park and tried to do a cartwheel. But when her hands touched the floor, she didn't move sideways. She simply stood on her hands.

"Wow," cried Abby. "That's a perfect handstand!"

Sophia laughed happily. It seemed that she was good at something, after all.